W9-DAO-766

LEESE WEBSTER

DISCARD

Atheneum Books by Ursula K. Le Guin

The Tombs of Atuan
The Farthest Shore
Very Far Away From Anywhere Else
Leese Webster

7/80
WLS
4"⁷⁷

JF
G

40971

LEESE WEBSTER

Story by Ursula K. Le Guin

Illustrated by James Brunsman

Atheneum   1979   New York

LIBRARY OF CONGRESS CATALOGING IN PUBLICATION DATA

Le Guin, Ursula K   Leese Webster.

SUMMARY: A palace spider's extraordinary webs,
which imitate paintings and carvings, take a new turn
when she is thrown out into the garden.
[1. Spiders—Fiction]   I. Brunsman, James
II. Title
PZ7.L5215Le   [E]   79-10424
ISBN 0-689-30715-2

Story copyright © 1979 by Ursula K. Le Guin
Illustrations copyright © 1979 by James Brunsman
All rights reserved
Published simultaneously in Canada by McClelland & Stewart, Ltd.
Manufactured by The Book Press, Brattleboro, Vermont
First Edition

For Philippa and Charles

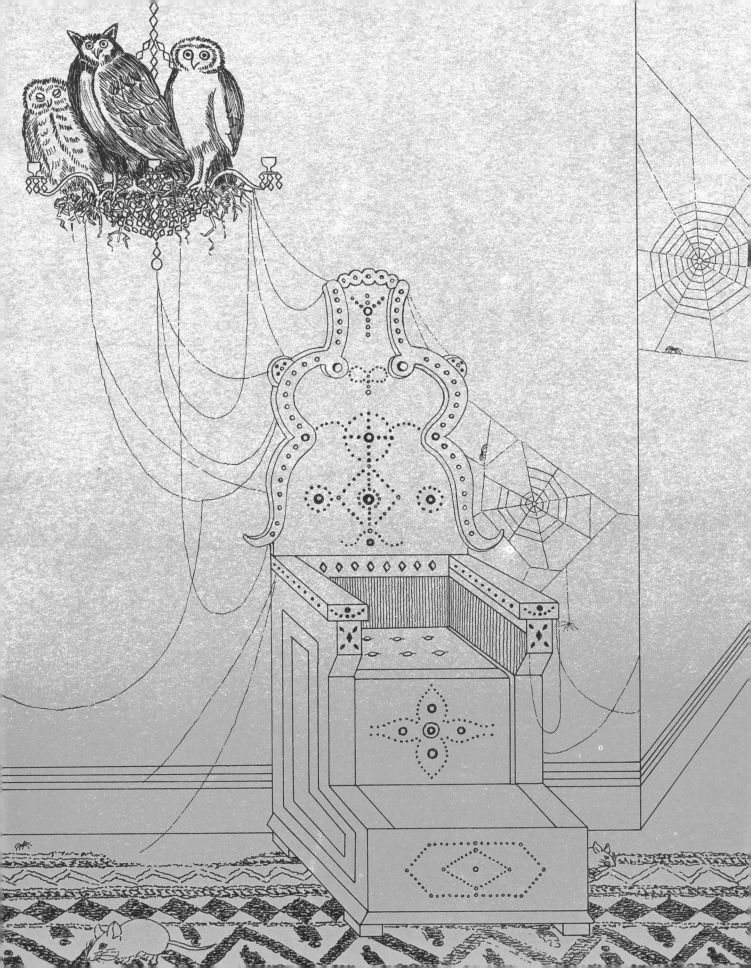

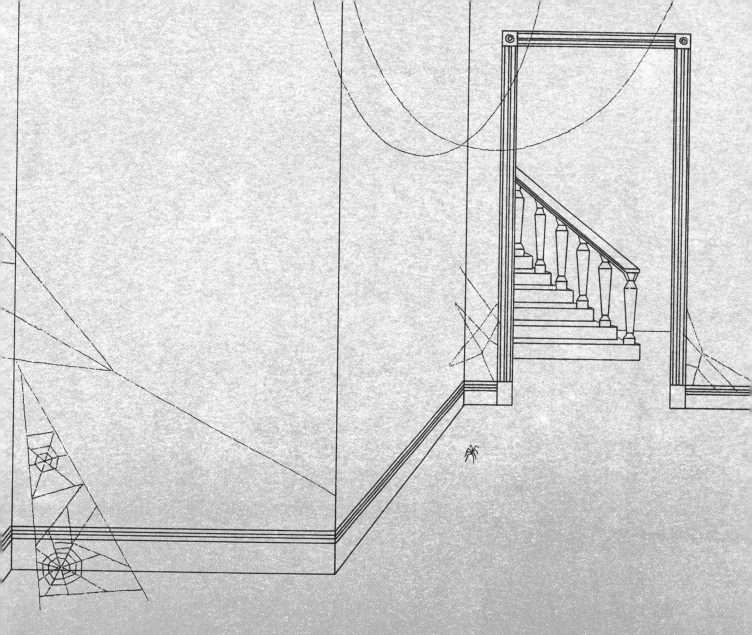

In a deserted palace, in the throne room where mice nested in the tattered carpeting and owls lived in the chandeliers and the throne itself was festooned with ropes of ancient cobweb, black with dust, a family of spiders hatched out one day. As soon as they had all said "Hello" to one another, they all said "Goodbye," and each went off to find a place to spin a web.

One of them, whose name was Leese, wandered about the throne room for a day or two. Finding all the corners occupied, she decided to go exploring. Along the ruined hallways of the palace she travelled, up the marble stairs, walking about on walls and ceilings as well as on the floors, discovering the undersides of things, creeping under the closed doors. About the time she was getting tired of exploring, she reached a comfortable room, the bedroom of a princess long ago. She found that she had the room pretty much to herself, which was the way she liked it; so she settled down there. And she began to spin.

The family Leese belonged to, the Websters, generally weave this kind of web:

It is a beautiful and practical design, and every member of the family knows how to weave it without giving it a thought. Leese wove such a web the first night in her new room. The second night, she wove another one, exactly the same. The third night, she said to herself, "I wonder why a web can't be a little different now and then?"

Her experiments did not work, at first. She kept learning and practicing, thinking out new ways to connect the threads, new patterns and new shapes. There were carved wooden cornices over the windows, a dark old painting on the wall, a threadbare carpet on the floor. She studied these and copied designs from them.

Most days, after she had traveled about the cornices and paintings for a while, she would curl up on a windowsill, in the warmth that came through the thick dust on the windowpanes, and plan what she might weave that night. Spiders like best to work in the dark, in the short, warm nights of summer.

To make the first, high thread to hold the web, she had to climb up high and then throw herself out across the dark air, hoping she would land safe on the other side. Her work was like riding the flying trapeze in the circus. It was like building bridges, too, because each part of the web helped hold up every other part in the air. And it was like singing, because she spun her thread out of her body, as the singer spins her voice out of her throat. As the singer's voice runs up and down the music, la-la-la!, so the patterns of Leese's thread ran up and down and round in lovely curves and angles. She had learned how to weave her ideas, now. Some of her webs had designs like leaves and flowers, imitated from the carpet; some had designs like huntsmen, hounds, and horns, copied from the painting on the wall.

Spiders are not sociable people. They mostly let one another be. Once in a great while other spiders, from the Webster family or other families, came through Leese's room and stared at her webs a while. Usually they sniffed, and traveled on.

Once one of them said, "That's a remarkable web you're weaving."

"Thank you," Leese said modestly.

"Will it catch flies?" the other spider asked.

"Not very well," said Leese. "The old pattern works better for that."

"Waste of time," said the other spider, and went on.

Leese was offended and a little ashamed. She improved her designs after that, so that her fancy webs would catch flies as well as the old kind. For that is the purpose of a spiderweb, after all, and spiders have to eat, like anybody else.

No matter what kind of web she wove, she did not eat very often. The balustrades and picture frames and panels of the deserted palace, the carvings and cornices and corners, were such good places for webs that for a hundred years the spiders had been spinning there. But the flies were few and far between, for there was nothing much to bring them. Leese was used to going hungry; she liked her lonely room; she would have been quite content, but for one thing. She was never quite satisfied with the webs she wove.

In the throne room where she had been born, on the arms and back of the empty throne, there had been jewels: stones that shone red, yellow, green, blue, violet, though they were dim with dust. In her memory those jewels were more beautiful than anything she could weave, for there was light inside them.

She wove jewel-shapes and jewel-patterns in her web, but the thread she spun was grey. She could not catch the colors of the light, as those stones caught it. "How do they do it?" she wondered.

One afternoon she felt a great commotion in the air, banging and thumping and voices calling. "It's a thunderstorm," she told herself, though it was a mild and sunny day. She had worked hard all night trying to weave a jewel and was sleepy; and spiders don't pay much attention to what goes on at a distance, anyhow. She curled her legs up and slept on, until a draft of air woke her suddenly, making all the threads of her webs tremble and sway.

Someone had opened the door of the room, for the first time in a hundred years.

"More cobwebs," said a disgusted voice. "Bring in the brooms!"

"Wait," said another voice. "Look!"

Leese scrambled up into the dustiest corner of the ceiling, behind the rags of one of her first practice webs, and listened in great fear. The word "broom" was the worst word she knew.

Two human beings came into the room. They were cleaning women, with mops and ladders and feather dusters. The old palace was being cleaned up and made into a National Monument, a museum where people could come and see how kings used to live.

"Tsk, tsk, tsk," said the first one, shaking her head sadly. "Look at those beautiful tapestries hanging about, but all so dusty and spiderwebby!"

"The tapestries are spiderwebs," said the second one.

"Spiders can't make pictures, dear," said the first one, laughing. But the second one, whose eyes were keener, said, "Oh, don't touch them—they *are* spiderwebs!"

Both women stood there among the wonderful webs, which shimmered a little in the draft from the open door.

"How beautiful they are," said the first one in a low voice.

"You stay here and keep the sweepers out," said the second one. "I'll go tell the Authorities!" And she went hurrying down the marble stairs.

The cleaning women would let the Authorities into the room only two at a time, ordering them to walk very carefully and NOT TO TOUCH. When all the Authorities had seen the webs, they held a conference and consulted experts.

The Experts on Tapestries were extremely puzzled and talked a great deal about looms, wefts, and bobbins. The Experts on Spiders argued with each other and were not very helpful. But all the experts agreed that the Room of the Silver Weavings (which is what the cleaning women named it) should be kept exactly as it was, so that visitors to the Palace Museum could see the remarkable tapestries.

"They are very delicate. Even dust gathering on them will tear them," said an Expert on Ancient Textiles.

So the experts agreed that the weavings must be kept under glass.

The next day, just as Leese had got comfortably to sleep in a warm corner of the windowsill, a whole new troop of human beings came into her room and began putting frames and panes of glass over all her finest webs.

"Stop!" Leese cried, rushing up and down the window-frame, careless of danger. "Stop that!"

But what human being ever listened to a spider?

"Stop that! If you cover my webs with glass, how can they catch flies?" Leese shouted. "I'll starve!"

The workmen paid no attention.

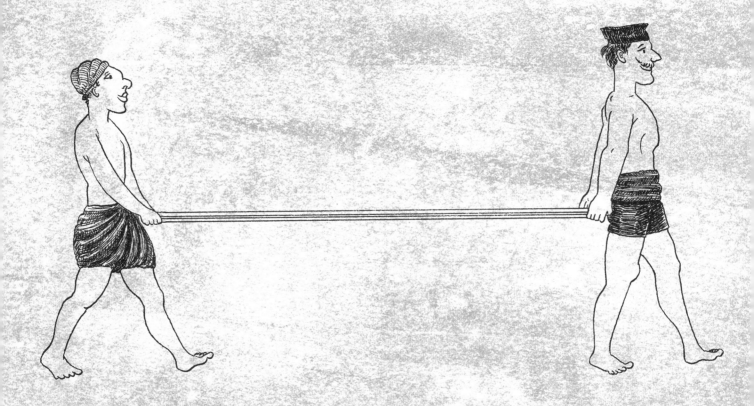

When all the Silver Weavings were neatly framed and glassed, the workmen left; and the two cleaning women came back.

They walked from frame to frame, admiring.

"This one's so pretty. Look at the horses and hounds," said the first one, while the second one was saying, "Oh, look at this one, the tiny leaves and flowers!"

They were proud of what they had found and happy to have saved it, and Leese was proud and happy to have her work admired at last.

"They say a thousand tourists will come here every day in summer," said the first cleaning woman.

"Will they bring flies with them?" thought Leese, hopefully.

"The experts all say there's nothing like these tapestries in the whole, wide world," said the second cleaning woman.

"I could have told you that," thought Leese.

"Well," said the first cleaning woman, "let's get the corners dusted and the windows polished. The Museum will be open to the public tomorrow morning."

And they opened up their stepladders, shook out their feather dusters, and began to dust the high corners of the room, behind the carvings, above the window frames, in the darkest crevices.

"Oh!" cried the first one, "there's a spider."

"Don't be frightened," said the second one, who was afraid of spiders. "Shake it off and step on it."

"Never kill a spider," said the first one. "It's bad luck." She shook her duster gently out the open window. "There, let go, little creepy. You'll catch more flies outside!"

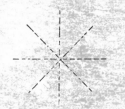

Leese spun out her thread desperately, but it would not stick to the shaking duster. She flew through the bright air, a farther fall than ever she had swung spinning, and landed on a broad, sunlight-speckled leaf. "I'm dead!" she cried, and lay there in a tiny ball, her legs curled tight, her eyes all shut.

The sun went down. The cool, damp, shadowy evening came into the palace gardens.

Leese opened one of her eight eyes.

"What's that?" she thought.

It was the evening star, reflected in the water of the lily pool. Leese, who had lived all her life indoors behind dirty windows, and was nearsighted anyway, had never seen the stars.

"It's a jewel," she thought. "And I'm not dead after all." She opened the other seven eyes and stretched her legs cautiously. "What a big room this is! It seems not to have any walls at all."

She walked about on her leaf and explored several other leaves and branches and a large white flower. She was on a camellia bush.

"This room is splendidly decorated already," she thought. "I scarcely know what to weave for it. But I am hungry—I am very hungry."

She attached a thread to the topmost leaf of the camellia bush, took a deep breath, and flung herself out into the air.

She caught the end of a branch of roses. Her thread held, and from it she wove a web. It was not a neat one, for she was tired and hungry, and the wind blew, and the branches moved. But all night long whenever she looked up from her work she saw the reflections of the stars in the water of the pool, among the lily flowers. "This must be a throne room," she thought.

As the dawn came, dew began to gather on her web.

Leese was distressed. She tried to shake the water beads off, for she did not know what they were. She twitched the threads of her web, but the tiny drops clung. Then the sun came up. The light of sunrise struck the drops of water strung close on every thread, and they shone brighter than the jewels of the throne, brighter even than the stars.

Breakfast came buzzing by. Leese ate it thankfully, while she watched her web glittering with diamond water beads. "That's the most beautiful web I ever wove," she thought.

Tourists came to the Palace Museum, hundreds of them every day. They all climbed up the marble stairs to the Room of the Silver Weavings, and they said, "How beautiful!" and, "Ah!" and, "Why, they're as fine as spiderwebs, aren't they?"

But Leese, swinging joyously from leaf to branch in the endless garden, wove her wild webs every night, and every morning found them shining with the jewels of the sun.